Dec. 2016

Dear Dianne —

Somehow 2016 fit the
title of this book!

All best wishes for a fantastic

2017 — all my love to my BFF —

Kathy

Written by Sue Salvi
Illustrated by Megan Kellie

For Augie and Oscar.
Go forth and be pooped on.

YOUR LIFE

I'm not the sort of person who can see into the future, but I do know that sometime in the long life you have ahead of you, there will be a day when a bird will poop on you.

Because there are birds up in the sky.

And because there are people down
below the sky.

And because you are one of those people.

So it just makes sense that someday you'll
feel something land on your head,

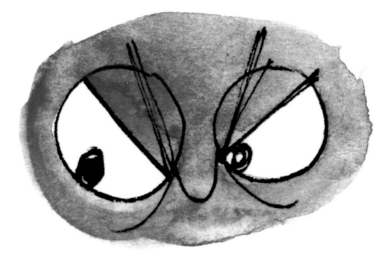

or on your shoulder,

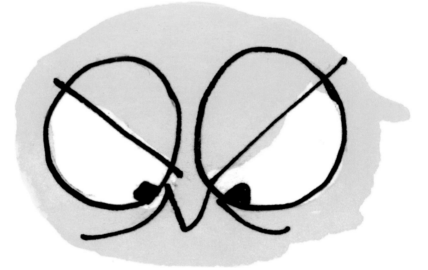

or down your lapel,

if it's a lapel-wearing kind of day,

and you'll reach for it
and feel the goo that is bird poo.

Probably every single day,
somewhere in the world,

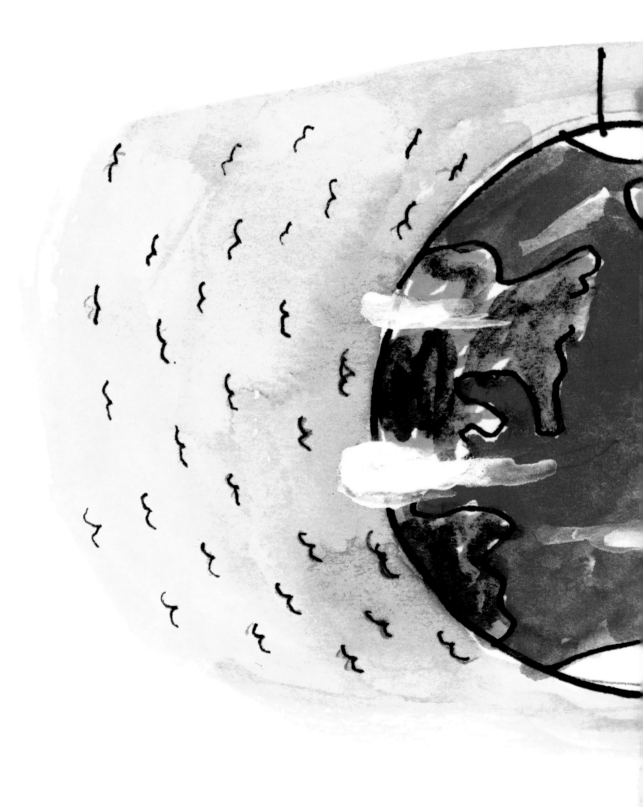

someone is getting pooped on by a bird.

Maybe right now even,
as this book is happening
to you,

someone in China is
getting pooped on by a
Chinese bird.

Or someone in Mexico is getting pooped on by a Mexican bird.

Or someone in Maine is getting pooped on by a visiting Canadian bird.

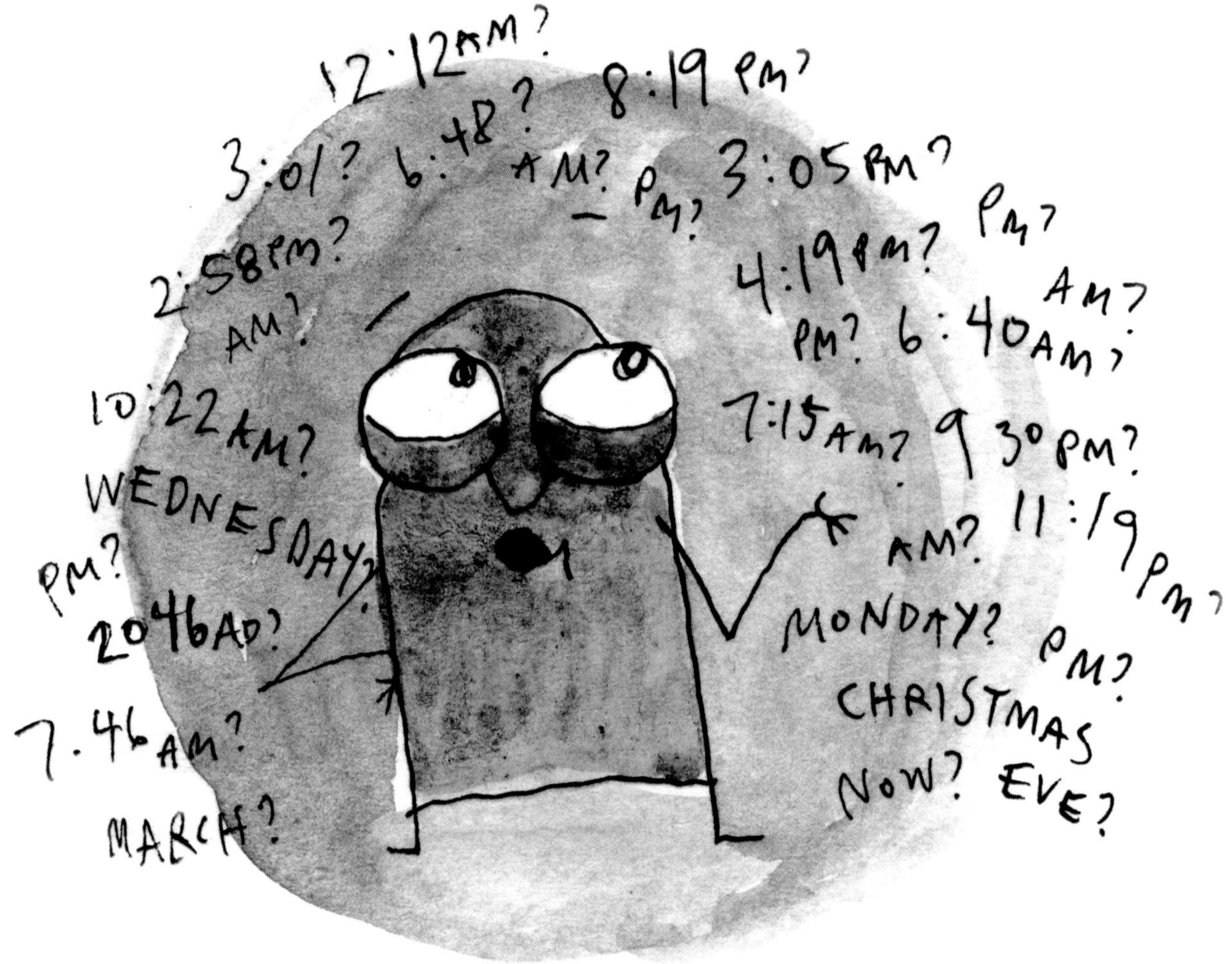

It just happens. You won't know when.

Other than it will be at the worst possible time it could happen.

Like a day you're wearing important clothes for a job interview.

Or a day you're running late for a ceremony during which you are to receive an award for never being late to anything.

That's how it happens.

It won't be on a day that you leave your house thinking, "Today I'm sure a bird will poop on me so I'll bring a change of clothes and leave early and I'll bring some bird toilet paper."

So, on the day that the bird
poops on you, you have two choices:

You can get really mad and cry
and stomp and say,

"I don't want this to happen,
raah, grahh, kerrrrr!"

And let it ruin the rest of your day.

Or...

You can remain calm, wash it off,
laugh about it and think to yourself,

"Now, chances are, I won't have
another bird poop on me for a while."

And if they do?

What a hilarious story that will be!

The End.

Sue Salvi, *Author*

Sue cherishes the bird poops she has received including a monstrous fecal incident that happened on her left forearm, moments before speaking at an extra-sacred church event. Originally from Pittsburgh, PA, Sue now lives in Chicago with her husband and two boys. She occasionally performs improv and sketch comedy around town. There has been a peregrine falcon in her backyard, twice so far. You may find her verbal poops @suesalvi.

Megan Kellie, *Illustrator*

Megan is proud of the bird poops she has collected while on earth. Once, sitting in a park, she thought, "wow, it's like I'm in a brochure" until a bird pooped on her, to let her know she was not. She lives in Chicago, is also a writer performer person, would like to make approximately everything, and prefers low ceilinged restaurants. She emits words @flipflipflap and drawings @spazzyhandclap.

Special thanks to Paul Grondy, R.T. Durston, Heather Skomba, John Bleeden, Julie Regimand and Ron Lazzeretti.